**W9-CDO-500**

DISCARD

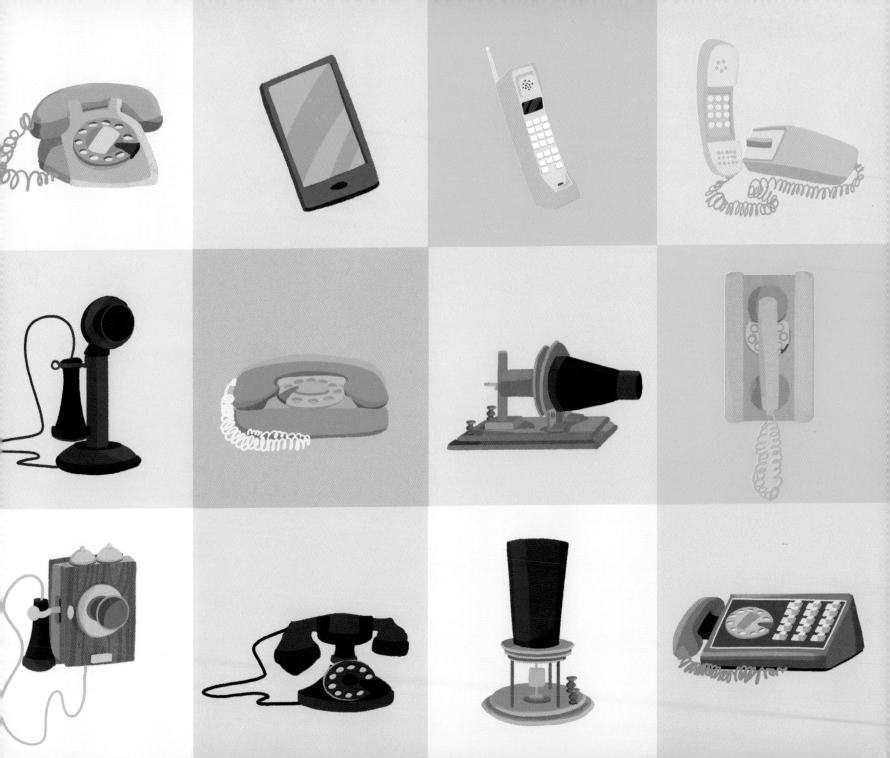

PHONES
KEEP US CONNECTED

BY KATHLEEN WEIDNER ZOEHFELD · ILLUSTRATED BY KASIA NOWOWIEJSKA

HARPER
An Imprint of HarperCollinsPublishers

Special thanks to Dr. Jerry Gibson, Distinguished Professor, Department of Electrical and Computer Engineering at the University of California, Santa Barbara, for his valuable assistance.

The Let's-Read-and-Find-Out Science book series was originated by Dr. Franklyn M. Branley, Astronomer Emeritus and former Chairman of the American Museum of Natural History–Hayden Planetarium, and was formerly co-edited by him and Dr. Roma Gans, Professor Emeritus of Childhood Education, Teachers College, Columbia University. Text and illustrations for each of the books in the series are checked for accuracy by an expert in the relevant field. For more information about Let's-Read-and-Find-Out Science books, write to HarperCollins Children's Books, 195 Broadway, New York, NY 10007, or visit our website at www.letsreadandfindout.com.

Let's Read-and-Find-Out Science® is a trademark of HarperCollins Publishers.

Phones Keep Us Connected
Text copyright © 2017 by Kathleen Weidner Zoehfeld
Illustrations copyright © 2017 by HarperCollins Publishers
All rights reserved. Manufactured in China.
No part of this book may be used or reproduced in any manner whatsoever without written permission except in the case of brief quotations embodied in critical articles and reviews. For information address HarperCollins Children's Books, a division of HarperCollins Publishers, 195 Broadway, New York, NY 10007.
www.harpercollinschildrens.com

ISBN 978-0-06-238668-7 (trade bdg.) — ISBN 978-0-06-238667-0 (pbk.)

The artist used Adobe Photoshop CC to create the digital illustrations for this book.
Typography by Erica De Chavez
16 17 18 19 20 SCP 10 9 8 7 6 5 4 3 2 1 ❖ First Edition

R0448400751

For Beth, Connie, Martha,
Nina, Sue, and Wendy—may
we always stay connected.
—K.Z.

For Filip, Marta, and Piotr,
my great friends
—K.N.

You asked your friend to meet you at the soccer game.
There she is—WAY across on the other side of the field.
"Over here!" you shout.
But your friend doesn't hear you. You're too far away.

No problem. Just grab your phone
and give her a call.
You and your friend are connected!

It doesn't matter how far away your friend is. You can always say hello! But it wasn't always that way. Before phones were invented, if you wanted to wish your friend a happy birthday, you could mail her a card. But there was no way she could hear your voice, unless you went to visit her.

Whenever you speak, you make the vocal cords in your throat **vibrate**. Those vibrations set the air around them vibrating, too. The vibrations move through the air in waves, called **sound waves**.

A loud sound has a lot of energy. But no matter how loud a sound is to begin with, the waves can only go so far before they begin to run out of energy and fade. People tried all kinds of ways to send their voices farther.

Did You Know?

Sound waves need something to travel through—such as air or water or even a solid object. If you clap your hands in outer space, a person right next to you wouldn't be able to hear it, since the sound would have nothing to travel through.

In the early 1800s, a few scientists discovered that sound could be sent along a straight wire. The solid wire helped the sound waves travel better than they do through air. You can do an experiment yourself, to find out how this works.

Make a String Telephone

You'll need:
- Measuring tape
- A ball of string
- Scissors
- Two paper cups
- A large needle

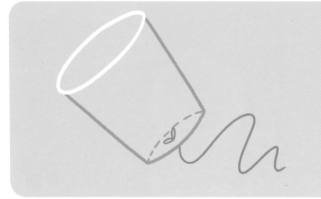

- Measure and cut a piece of string about 10 feet (3 meters) long.
- Use the needle to poke a small hole in the center of the bottom of each cup.
- Thread one end of the string through the bottom of one cup and make a small knot in the string to keep it from pulling out.
- Then do the same with the other cup.

When participating in activities in this book, it is important to keep safety in mind. Several experiments in the book call for the use of sharp objects. Children should always ask permission from an adult before doing any of the activities and should be supervised by an adult at all times. The publisher, author, and artist disclaim any liability from any injury that might result from the participation, proper or improper, of the activities contained in this book.

Have your friend hold one cup, and you hold the other. Stretch the string out between you, gently, until it is straight and tight.

Have your friend hold her cup up to her ear while you quietly say something into your cup. Then say the same words to her, without the string phone. Which way did your friend hear you better?

When you speak into the cup, the sound of your voice makes the air in the cup vibrate. And that makes the bottom of the cup vibrate. The vibrations move quickly through the string. That makes the bottom of the other cup vibrate in the same way as the bottom of your cup. Those vibrations become sound waves that travel through the air in your friend's cup. And she hears your voice, as if you were right up close.

A wire or string phone might help people talk to each other in the same house. But it didn't solve the big problem: how to make the sound of your voice travel FAR!

In the 1830s, inventors figured out how to use the energy of electricity to send coded messages. The new invention was called the electrical telegraph. Samuel Morse created a simple code of dots and dashes.

Happy Birthday

Wires were strung up all around the world. People were amazed by how fast and how far electricity could carry their messages.

It wasn't long before some people, such as Alexander Graham Bell, started wondering: Could electricity be used to carry the human voice over long distances, too?

Bell was a speech teacher. He spent most of his time helping deaf children learn to talk. What Bell wanted more than anything was for people to be able to speak to and understand each other. He didn't know a lot about electricity. But he studied and learned as much about it as he could.

In 1876, he and his assistant, Thomas Watson, were working on improving the telegraph when they made an interesting discovery. One of the metal springs on Watson's telegraph got stuck to its magnet. He plucked it loose.

"Twang!" went the spring.

Over in the next room, Bell's telegraph was connected to Watson's. And Bell heard the spring on his telegraph twang, too!

"What did you do?" shouted Bell.

"I plucked the spring," said Watson.

"Do it again!" cried Bell.

Watson did. Again, the spring in Bell's telegraph made the same twanging sound.

From that point on, Bell knew that an electrical current could carry a complex sound. If it could do that, maybe it really could carry the human voice!

17

Bell and Watson were finally ready to build their first phone. Here's how it worked:

TRANSMITTER:
This is the part that sends, or transmits, your voice.

Mouthpiece:
You speak into the opening of the mouthpiece.

Diaphragm:
A very thin sheet of metal that vibrates easily—like the bottom of the paper cup in your string telephone experiment!

Wire:
The wire carries the electrical signal to the receiver.

Magnet:
A magnet is attached to the diaphragm. When the diaphragm vibrates, it makes the magnet vibrate. The vibrating magnet causes a wavy, vibrating flow of electricity.

RECEIVER:
This is the part that gets, or receives, your voice.

Earpiece:
You put your ear against the opening in the earpiece.

Diaphragm:
The diaphragm turns the electrical signal back into sound waves.

Wire:
The electrical waves made by the magnet pulse through the wire in a pattern. The pattern is exactly like the pattern of sound waves made by your voice.

Bell and Watson kept experimenting. They soon knew there were two ways to change sound into electricity. One was to use a moving magnet to create the vibrating flow of electricity. That's how they made their first phone. But they weren't very happy with its sound.

Battery-powered transmitter

Acid cup

Receiver

So they tried the second way. They used a battery to create a steady flow of electricity through the wires. They set up the transmitter so that the vibrations of the diaphragm would make the strength of that electrical flow vary. The varying strength of the electrical flow would match the pattern of sound waves made by your voice. This new phone's sound was much clearer.

From the start, the battery-powered phone worked better than the moving-magnet phone. But Bell's phone needed a small, open cup of acid in order to work. Building and using it was not easy—or safe!

Thomas Edison worked on the problem. He made a small packet filled with little grains of carbon that could be used instead of the acid. Of all the inventions for making phones easy to build and use, Edison's worked best.

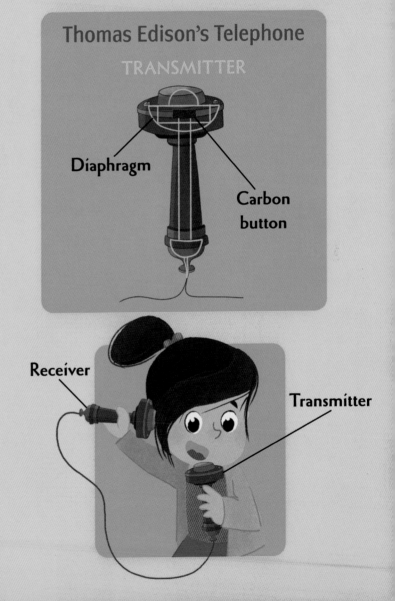

Thomas Edison's Telephone
TRANSMITTER

Diaphragm

Carbon button

Receiver

Transmitter

Wires had already been strung up everywhere for telegraphs. Telegraph poles were quickly put to use to string up wires for the new telephones. For the first time, people far away from one another could have conversations. We were connected!

Even today, the transmitters and receivers in phones work very much like they did in the time of Bell and Edison. But those phones needed wires.

You can call up your friend when she's on the other side of the soccer field. Or anywhere else you can think of! How do you send your voice across many miles, without any wires?

Instead of wires, your cell phone uses a form of energy called radio waves.

Not long after the first telephones were invented, Heinrich Hertz and others began experimenting with radio waves.

To send a radio broadcast, you need an antenna. That's a device that can create radio waves by generating back-and-forth bursts of electricity. Then you need a microphone. This is like a telephone's transmitter. It turns the sound waves into an electrical signal. That signal makes small changes in the radio waves—in a pattern exactly matching the vibrations of your voice. The radio waves carry the signal out.

Lots of people can listen to your radio broadcast. Your friend is one of your biggest fans, so he has his radio tuned to pick up your show's radio waves. His radio's receiver—like the telephone's receiver—turns them back into an electrical signal. And his radio's built-in speaker—like the phone's diaphragm—turns the signal into the sound of your voice.

Radio Waves

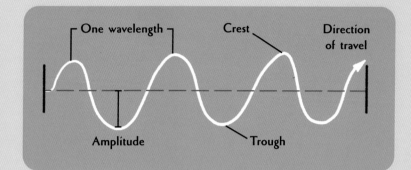

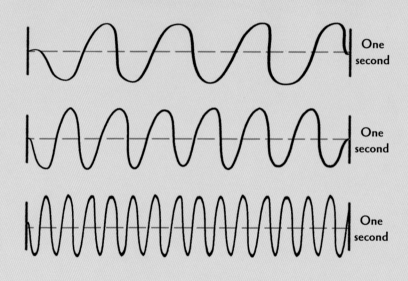

Waves have ups and downs—called crests and troughs. The distance between two crests is the wavelength. The number of ups and downs that occur each second is the **frequency** of the wave. Each radio station's antenna sends out its waves at a particular frequency. You can tune your radio to pick up the frequency of your favorite station.

Your cell phone is like a tiny radio station. It has a small built-in antenna. It can send out radio waves. And it can receive them, too.

A battery gives your phone its power. The phone uses this power to create radio waves. But how can your little phone connect to a phone that is thousands of miles away? It doesn't have to. It only has to send to or receive from the nearest cellular antenna.

That antenna can send your signal out to a switching center, where it travels through wires or optical fiber to a switching center closer to your friend. From there it is sent to the cellular antenna nearest to your friend's phone.

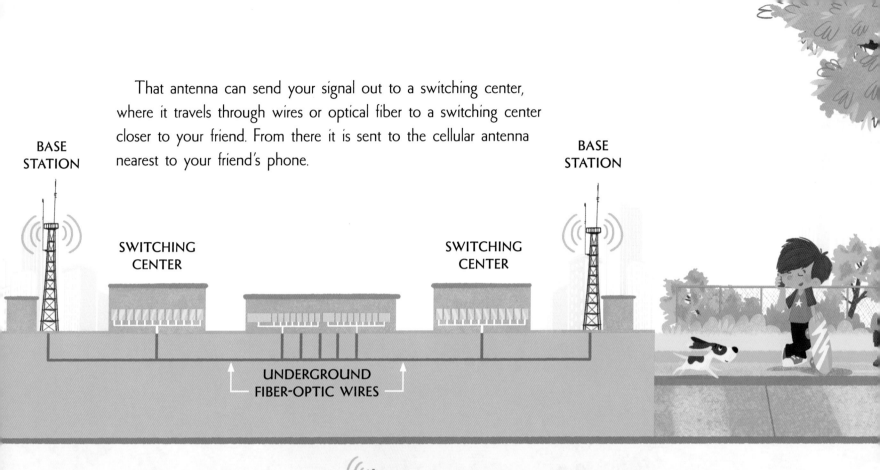

BASE STATION

SWITCHING CENTER

SWITCHING CENTER

BASE STATION

UNDERGROUND FIBER-OPTIC WIRES

Even when you call your friend at the soccer field, the radio waves carrying your voice do not go straight to your friend's phone. They first travel to the nearest cellular antenna and then to his phone.

Like the phones of Bell and Edison, your cell phone changes your voice into an electrical signal. But your cell phone has a new addition. It has a built-in computer. The computer changes that electrical signal into computer code.

INSIDE VIEW OF YOUR PHONE

Speaker (Receiver)

Antenna

Computer

Battery

Microphone (Transmitter)

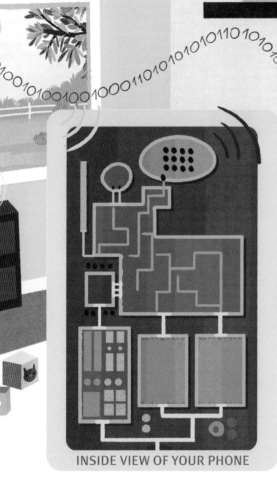

INSIDE VIEW OF YOUR PHONE

Back in the 1970s, the first wireless phones were as big as a brick and almost as heavy.

The pattern of the code makes small changes in the radio waves your phone sends out. The antenna nearest your friend picks up your code and sends it to his phone. The computer in his phone decodes it and turns it back into an electrical signal. And the receiver changes the signal into the sound of your voice.

Over the years, new inventions have made all the parts that make up your cell phone—from its battery and antenna to the electrical pathways on its computer chips—much smaller and lighter. That's why your phone is so small and yet can do so many things.

Alexander Graham Bell put together old discoveries about sound and electricity and he came up with a great new invention. A hundred years after Bell, inventors put together ideas about radio waves and the telephone and came up with another invention—the cell phone.

Scientists and inventors continue to put old discoveries together in new ways. But today we have many more discoveries and inventions to work with than Bell did!

What else do you wish your phone could do? Be sure to write down your ideas and draw sketches. That way you'll remember them. If you keep at it, you'll be able to develop your ideas over time and share them with others. Your new inventions will spring from the old inventions that have become a part of our everyday world.

Glossary

Antenna: A device used to send or receive radio, television, or cell phone signals. A sending antenna changes electrical energy into electromagnetic radiation. A receiving antenna does the opposite.

Carbon: A common element that is one of the building blocks of all living things. In nature, carbon can also be found in coal, in charcoal, and in graphite, which is used to make pencils.

Diaphragm: A very thin, usually disk-shaped object that vibrates easily when hit by sound waves.

Electricity: Electricity is a form of energy. It can be created by a battery or by a moving magnet or in a few other ways. Electricity can be made to flow through a wire. Electrical energy can be changed into other forms of energy.

Frequency: The number of up and down cycles per second of any wave motion.

Radio waves: Radio waves are one form of energy called electromagnetic radiation. Electromagnetic radiation is generated throughout the universe by the Sun and other stars. Light, heat, and X-rays are other types of electromagnetic radiation.

Receiver: A device that picks up, or receives, radio waves or electrical signals and turns them into sound waves.

Sound waves: Vibrations that move through air or through some other substance. All sound waves are created by a vibrating object of some kind.

Telegraph: Any device used to send messages across great distances. An electrical telegraph uses the energy of electricity to send its signals.

Transmitter: A device used to send out, or transmit, electrical signals or radio waves.

Vibrate: To move quickly, and continuously, back and forth or up and down. A vibrating object sets the air around it vibrating. And we hear the vibrations as sound.

FIND OUT MORE

Building a Better String Phone

Did you follow the instructions for building a string phone? How did it work? Do you wonder if you could make it work better? If so, then you have the mind of an inventor!

It's time to start experimenting! Make sure you have a notebook and pencil handy so you can keep track of your results.

Maybe you have some ideas for improving your phone already. If not, here are a few questions to get you started:

- Would my phone sound better if I used a different kind of string? You could try it out with yarn, fishing line, or thread.
- Would a longer string make the sound better or worse, or would the sound stay the same? Can I make my phone work with a *very* long string?
- Will my phone work if I bend the string around a corner? What about if someone holds on to the string in the center?
- The instructions said to stretch the string out until it is straight and tight. Why? What happens if you let the string hang loose? Is the sound better or worse or the same?

- Would my phone be easier to build if I used tape instead of small knots to hold the string on the bottoms of the cups? Will the tape make the sound better or worse, or will it stay the same?
- Maybe you'd like to make your phone look prettier. What will happen if I decorate the cups with paint or with construction paper and glue? Will the sound be better or worse or the same?

When you're done experimenting, draw a picture of your very own new and improved string phone in your notebook. Be sure to add labels and notes so you remember how you built it!

A Short History of the Phone

1876

The first telephone was invented by Alexander Graham Bell. "Mr. Watson—come here—I want to see you!" was the first sentence heard over the phone.

1900–1910

Telephones take off.

OF PHONES

Year	Millions
1900	0.6
1905	2.2
1910	5.8

1   2   3   4   5   6
(MILLIONS)

1919

Rotary dial phone was invented.

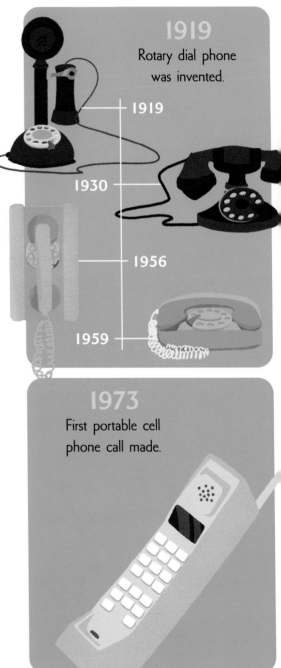

1919
1930
1956
1959

1927

The first two-way phone call that crossed an ocean was made..

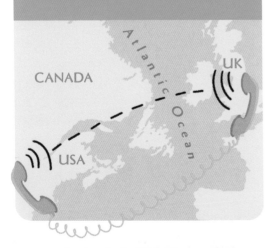

Atlantic Ocean

CANADA

UK

USA

1968

911 was chosen as the emergency number.

1973

First portable cell phone call made.

This book aligns with the Next Generation Science Standards.
Find out more at nextgenscience.org.

This book meets the Common Core State Standards for Science and
Technical Subjects. For Common Core resources for this title and others,
please visit www.readcommoncore.com.

Be sure to look for all of these books in the
Let's-Read-and-Find-Out Science series:

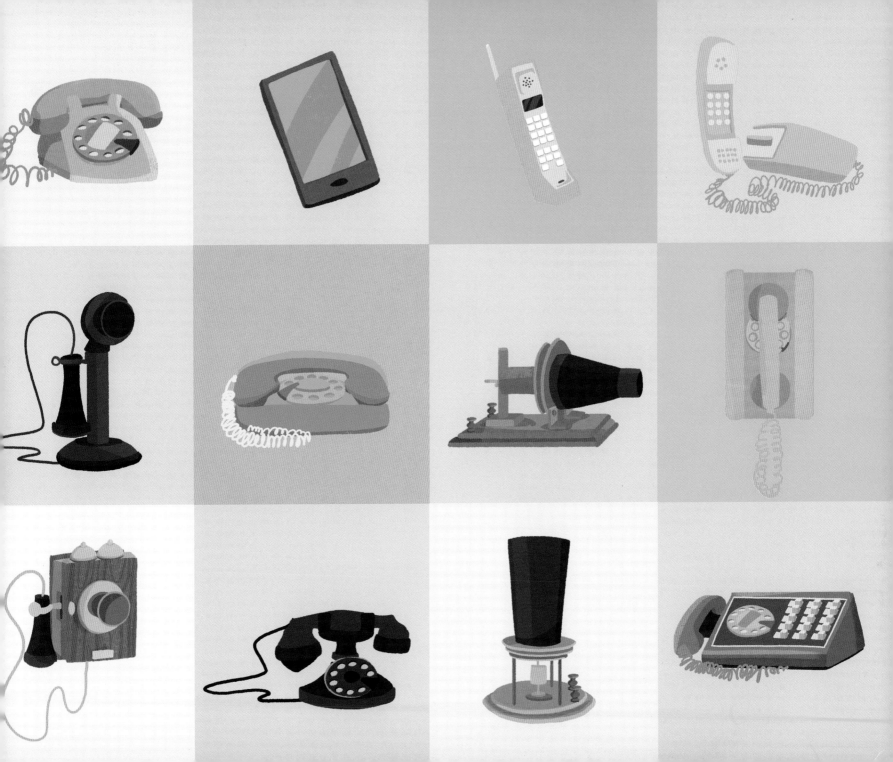

j611.71
JA752s

W9-CCI-723

AR RL 4.3 PY 0I

THE SKELETAL SYSTEM

EARLY BIRD
BODY SYSTEMS

BY CAROLINE ARNOLD

JUL   CHANEY BRANCH LIBRARY
2015   16101 GRAND RIVER
        DETROIT, MI 48227

LERNER PUBLICATIONS COMPANY • MINNEAPOLIS

CY

The photographs in this book are used with the permission of: © *PhotoDisc Royalty Free by Getty Images, pp. 5, 6, 7, 8, 10, 14, 18, 22, 23, 25, 27, 30, 31, 32, 34, 37, 39, 40, 46, 48 (bottom);* © *Todd Strand/Independent Picture Service, pp. 9, 19, 20, 33;* © *Royalty-Free/CORBIS, pp. 12, 15, 16, 24, 28, 36, 38, 42, 43, 47, 48 (top);* © *Stockbyte, p. 17; Agricultural Research Service, USDA, p. 21;* © *3Dclinic by Getty Images, p. 26;* © *Lester Lefkowitz/Taxi by Getty Images, p. 29.*

Cover photograph © *Royalty-Free/CORBIS.*

Text copyright © 2005 by Caroline Arnold

All rights reserved. International copyright secured. No part of this book may be reproduced, stored in a retrieval system, or transmitted in any form or by any means—electronic, mechanical, photocopying, recording, or otherwise—without the prior written permission of Lerner Publishing Group, Inc., except for the inclusion of brief quotations in an acknowledged review.

Lerner Publications Company
A division of Lerner Publishing Group, Inc.
241 First Avenue North
Minneapolis, MN 55401 U.S.A.

Website address: www.lernerbook.com

Library of Congress Cataloging-in-Publication Data

Arnold, Caroline.
      The skeletal system / by Caroline Arnold.
         p.   cm. — (Early bird body systems)
      Includes index.
      Summary: Explains how the different types of bones of the body work harmoniously together.
      ISBN-13: 978–0–8225–5140–9 (lib. bdg. : alk. paper)
      ISBN-10: 0–8225–5140–3 (lib. bdg. : alk. paper)
      1. Human skeleton—Juvenile literature. [1. Skeleton. 2. Bones.] I. Title. II. Series.
   QM101.A75 2005
   611'.71—dc22   2003023026

Manufactured in the United States of America
4 – BP – 11/1/09

CONTENTS

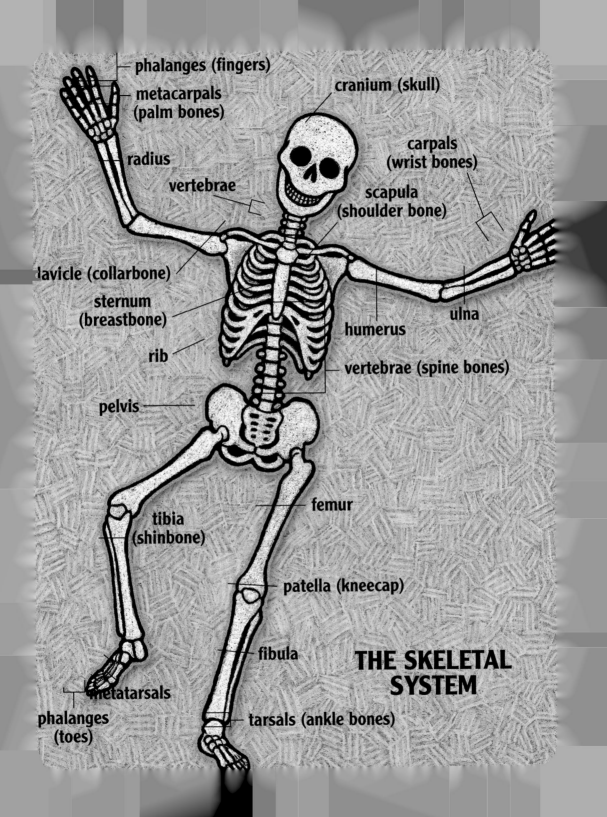

phalanges (fingers)

metacarpals
(palm bones)

radius

vertebrae

clavicle (collarbone)

sternum
(breastbone)

rib

pelvis

tibia
(shinbone)

metatarsals

phalanges
(toes)

cranium (skull)

carpals
(wrist bones)

scapula
(shoulder bone)

humerus

ulna

vertebrae (spine bones)

femur

patella (kneecap)

fibula

tarsals (ankle bones)

**THE SKELETAL
SYSTEM**

BE A WORD DETECTIVE

Can you find these words as you read about the skeletal system? Be a detective and try to figure out what they mean. You can turn to the glossary on page 46 for help.

blood vessels	marrow	skull
cartilage	nerves	spinal cord
enamel	organs	spine
joint	periosteum	tendons
ligaments	skeleton	vertebra

CHAPTER 1

THE BODY'S SUPPORT

You have bones in all parts of your body. Your bones support your body the way an umbrella's ribs support it.

Bones make up the body's skeletal system. You cannot see your bones. But you can feel them underneath your skin. You need bones to support and protect your body. Bones also help your body work.

Bones are hard and strong. Most other parts of the body are soft. Bones act like the poles inside a tent. They hold up your body and give it shape and support.

If you had no bones, you could not run, jump, or do cartwheels.

Bones and muscles work together. Muscles pull the bones to make them move. Muscles attached to your arm and leg bones help you run or throw a ball. Muscles attached to your finger bones help you write or pick up a spoon.

Bones protect organs inside your body. Your skull protects your brain. Your ribs form a cage around your heart and lungs. Your hip bones protect organs in the lower part of your body.

The muscles and bones of your hand work together to help you draw.

CHAPTER 2

Your bones help you stand up straight and tall. What is your longest bone?

WHAT IS A BONE?

Bones come in many sizes. Your smallest bone is in your ear. It is only about as big as a sesame seed. Your longest bone is in your upper leg. It is about one-fourth of your total height.

Bones come in many shapes. Long bones are found in your arms and legs. They usually have knobby ends and a straight central shaft. Short bones are found in your wrists and ankles. Your ribs, shoulder bones, breastbone, and the bones of your skull are flat bones. Bones of your spine and inner ear have odd, bumpy shapes.

The bones of your arms and legs are long bones. Bones in other parts of your body have many different shapes.

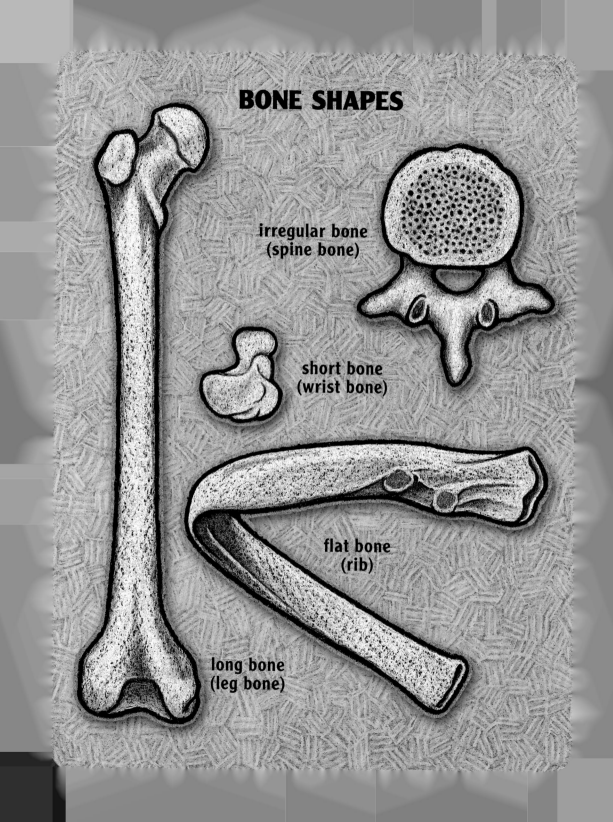

BONE SHAPES

irregular bone
(spine bone)

short bone
(wrist bone)

flat bone
(rib)

long bone
(leg bone)

Most of the surface of a bone is covered with a thin layer of blood vessels and nerves. This layer is called the periosteum (PAIR-ee-OHS-tee-uhm). The periosteum helps the bone grow and repair itself.

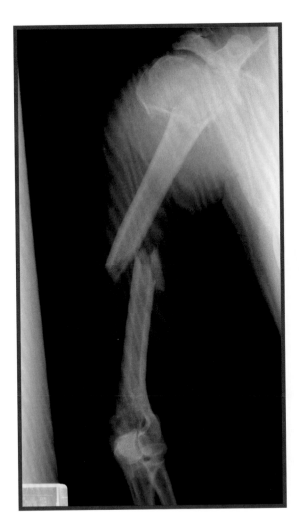

Bones are strong, but sometimes they break. This is an X-ray picture of a broken arm bone.

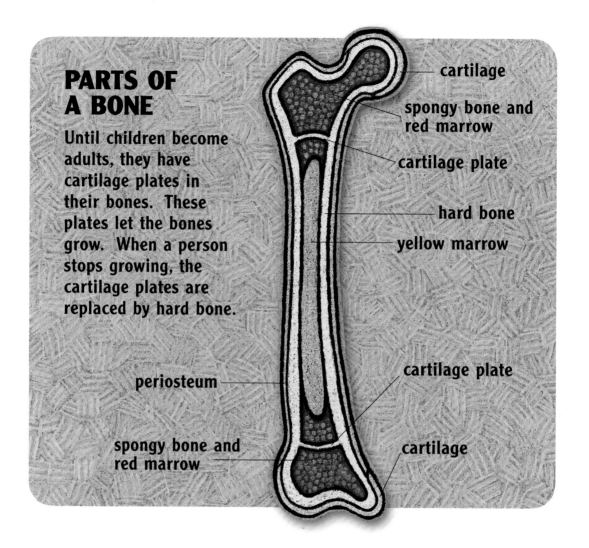

PARTS OF A BONE

Until children become adults, they have cartilage plates in their bones. These plates let the bones grow. When a person stops growing, the cartilage plates are replaced by hard bone.

cartilage

spongy bone and red marrow

cartilage plate

hard bone

yellow marrow

cartilage plate

periosteum

spongy bone and red marrow

cartilage

Beneath the periosteum is hard bone. Tiny holes in hard bone let blood vessels and nerves pass through. Under the hard bone is a layer of lighter, spongy bone. It looks something like a honeycomb.

Most bones have a soft jellylike material in the center. This material is called marrow. Yellow bone marrow stores fat. Red bone marrow makes blood cells. Your bones make thousands of new blood cells every day.

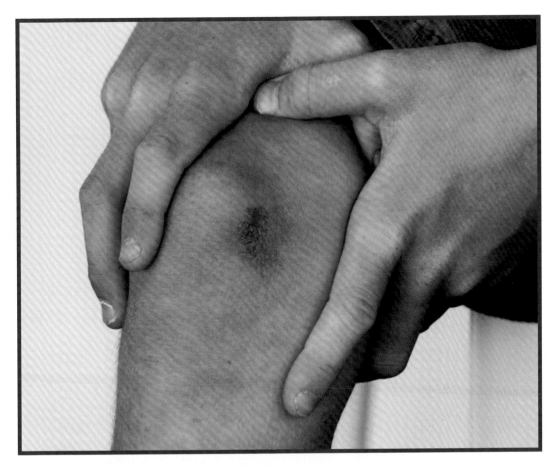

When you scrape your knee, sticky platelets in your blood form a scab to keep germs out. Platelets are made by red bone marrow.

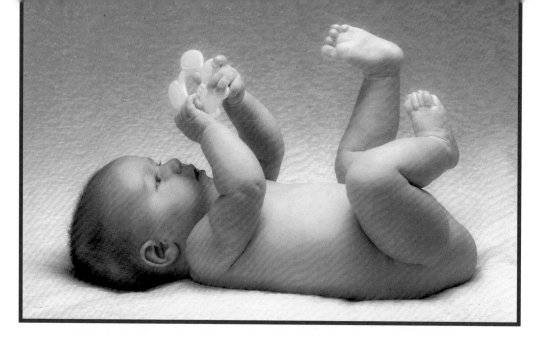

A newborn baby's body has about 300 bones. Some of them join together as the baby grows. An adult has about 206 bones.

The ends of most bones are covered with a white material called cartilage (KAR-tuh-lihj). Cartilage protects bones where they rub against each other. You also have cartilage in your nose and ears. Cartilage is tough and slippery and can bend a little. It is not as hard as bone, but it is strong. The bones of a baby's skeleton begin as cartilage. The cartilage is slowly replaced by hard bone as the child grows.

CHAPTER 3

YOUR SKELETON

The bones of your head are called your skull. How many bones make up your skull?

Your skeleton is the framework for your body. You could not stand up or move if you did not have a skeleton.

The skull is at the top of the skeleton. If you touch your head, your skull feels like one big smooth bone under the skin. But it is actually 29 bones joined together. Your skull acts like a built-in helmet. It protects the organs of your head.

The top of a baby's head has soft spots. These spots are spaces between the skull bones. The spaces fill up with bone by the time a baby is about two years old.

The top of the skull covers the brain. The bones at the front of the skull support the face. Put your hands on your face. Can you feel the holes in your skull around your eyes? Your skull also has a hole for your nose and two openings for your ears.

The front of your skull has 14 bones that support your face.

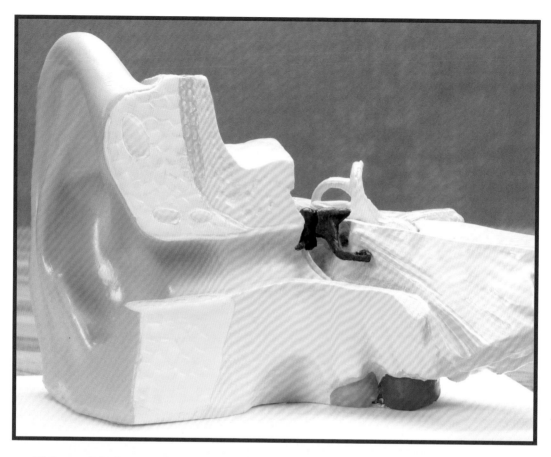

This model shows what the inside of a person's ear looks like. The three tiny ear bones are painted dark blue.

Each of your ears has three tiny bones inside. Sounds make these bones move. Nerves carry this information from your ear to your brain. Then you hear the sound.

The lower jawbone is the only part of the skull that can move. It moves up, down, and sideways. It helps you talk, bite, and chew.

Your lower jaw helps you bite into an apple.

Your baby teeth began to fall out when you were about six years old. Then permanent teeth started to grow in.

Your teeth are attached to the bones of your jaw. Teeth are even harder than bones. They are covered with a thick layer of a tough material called enamel (ih-NAM-uhl). Enamel protects your teeth from wearing down as you chew.

Your spine connects your skull to the rest of your body. The spine is a row of 33 bones. Each one is called a vertebra (VUHR-tuh-bruh). Together, they form a bony rod that supports your back.

Your back is made of hard bones. But the bones can move to let you bend over and touch your toes.

Your back twists to let you look back over your shoulder.

A single bone cannot bend. But the spine is like a row of beads on a wire. The row bends and twists as you move. A pad of cartilage cushions each vertebra.

The large, round part of each vertebra supports the body's weight. A hole through the center lets the spinal cord pass through. The spinal cord carries messages between the brain and other parts of the body. Muscles attach to bony spikes at the side and back of each vertebra. You can feel the knobs if you run your hand along your spine.

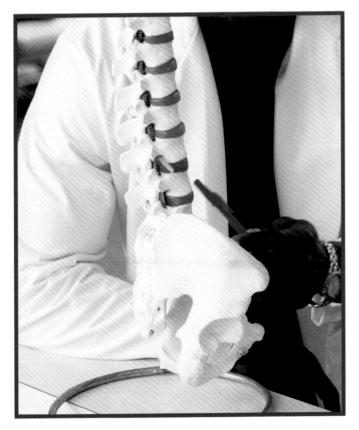

Between the bones of your back are pads of cartilage. The cartilage keeps the bones from rubbing together when you move.

Your ribs are just under the skin of your chest.

The ribs are long, flat bones curving around the chest. You have 12 sets of ribs. In the back, one end of each rib is attached to the spine. In the front of the body, all of the ribs except the bottom two pairs are attached to the breastbone. The bottom two pairs of ribs are called floating ribs.

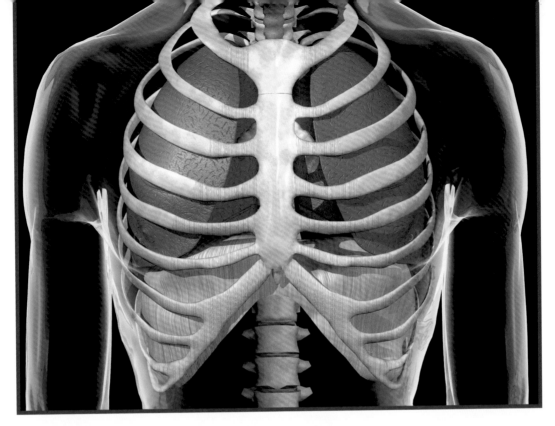

The ribs protect the organs of the upper body.

The ribs, spine, and breastbone make up the rib cage. It is like a fence around the upper body. The rib cage protects the heart, lungs, kidneys, liver, and other organs.

Your rib cage also helps you breathe. When muscles lift up your rib cage, air flows into your lungs. When the muscles relax, air goes out.

The bones of your arm are joined to the rest of your body at your shoulder. The shoulder bone is a strong, large, flat bone in your back. In the front, the shoulder is supported by the collarbone.

The two hard bumps on your back are your shoulder bones.

Your upper arm has one long bone. Your lower arm has two bones. Hold your lower left arm with your right hand and then turn your left wrist. Can you feel the bones twist? These bones move so you can carry things or throw a ball.

Your arm bones can twist to help you swing a bat.

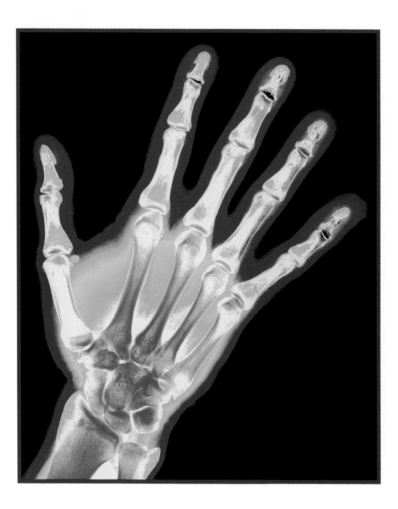

This picture shows the bones of the hand and wrist.

Your wrist is a group of small, knobby bones. These bones are connected to the five bones of your palm. Each of the palm bones is connected to the long bones of the fingers and thumb. You need your fingers and thumb to hold onto things.

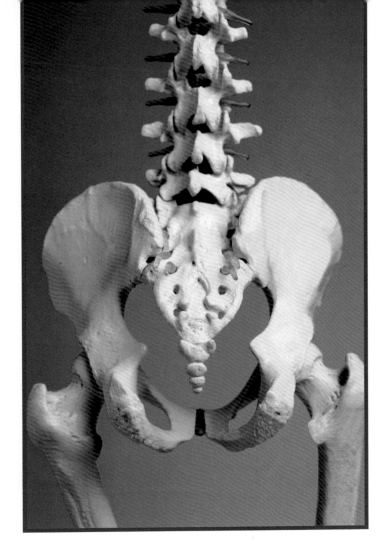

The hip bones are connected to the bottom of the spine.

The legs are connected to the rest of the body at the hips. The hip bones support the lower body and protect its organs. You can feel the top of your hip bones if you put your hand on your side just below your waist.

The upper leg has one large bone. The lower leg has two bones that can twist just like the bones of the lower arm. These bones let the lower leg turn.

Twisting leg bones let you sit cross-legged.

Do you ever fall and bump your knee? Your knee is covered by a small bone called the kneecap. It helps protect your knee.

When you kneel, your knees rest on the ground. Your kneecaps protect the ends of your leg bones.

The bones of your feet are much like the bones of your hands.

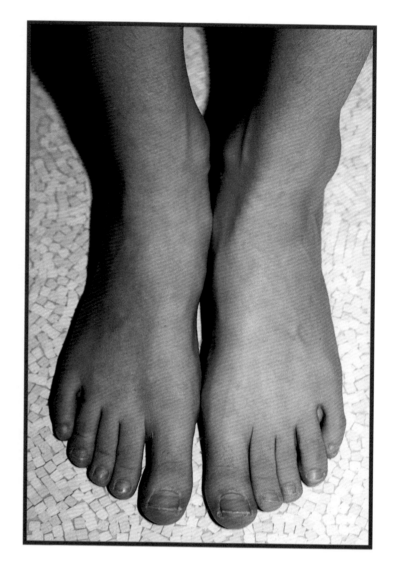

The bones of your feet are similar to the bones of your hands. But the foot bones cannot move as well. They are used mainly for standing, walking, and running.

CHAPTER 4

CONNECTING THE BONES

Bones are connected to make up the skeleton. What is the name of a place where two bones meet?

The place where two bones meet is called a joint. Different parts of the body have different kinds of joints.

KINDS OF MOVING JOINTS

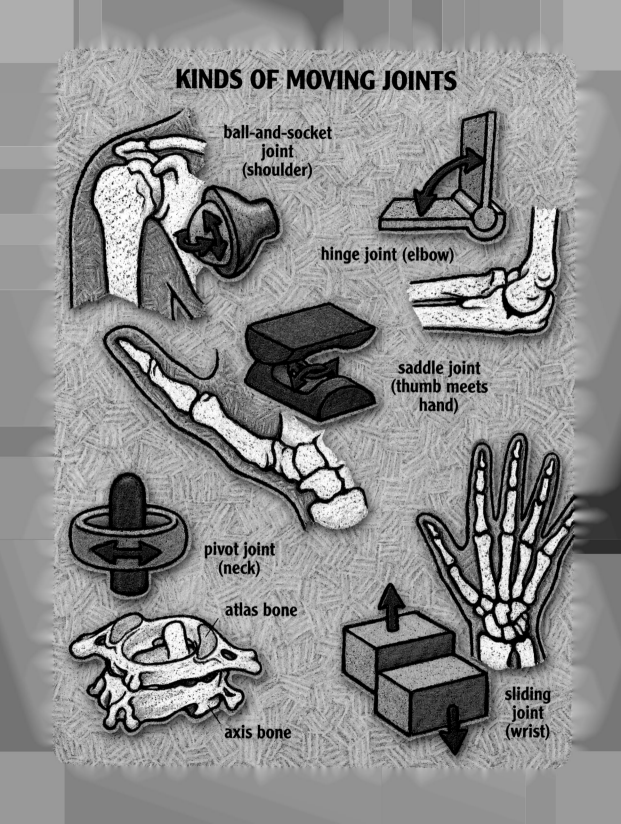

ball-and-socket joint (shoulder)

hinge joint (elbow)

saddle joint (thumb meets hand)

pivot joint (neck)

atlas bone

axis bone

sliding joint (wrist)

The ball-and-socket joint in your shoulder lets you raise your hand above your head.

Your shoulders and hips have ball-and-socket joints. The end of your arm or leg bone is round, like a ball. It fits into a cuplike shape in the shoulder bone or hip bone. Ball-and-socket joints let the arms and legs move in almost every direction.

The hinge joint in your elbow bends in only one direction.

The joints of your fingers bend in only one direction. These joints are called hinge joints. They work like the hinges on a door. You also have hinge joints in your knees and elbows.

The joint of the thumb is called a saddle joint. It is shaped like a riding saddle. This joint lets you move your thumb up and down and sideways. You also have saddle joints in your wrists and ankles.

You have a special pivot joint at the top of your spine. This joint is like a ring sitting on a peg. It lets your head move from side to side and nod up and down.

The bones of your spine are connected with gliding joints. These joints let the bones slide slightly when you bend your back. But they keep the spine stiff enough to hold up your body. You also have gliding joints in your wrists and ankles.

The pivot joint in your neck lets your head turn in many different directions.

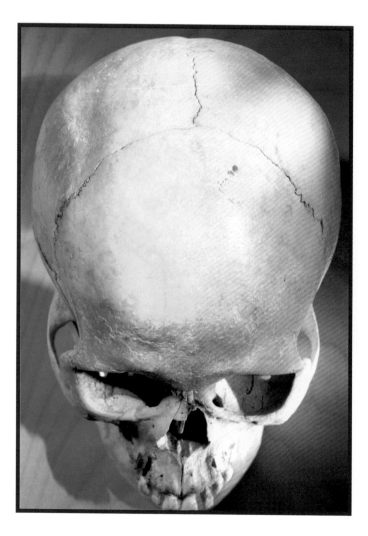

The zigzag lines on this skull are places where the different bones meet.

Some joints fasten bones together so they do not move at all. These joints are called suture joints. Your skull is held together by suture joints. They look like zigzag lines across the bone.

Muscles and bones work together.

Inside the joints that move is a liquid that helps the bones to slide easily against each other. This liquid works in the same way that oil helps a machine run smoothly.

Bones are connected with tough bands called ligaments (LIHG-uh-mehnts). Ligaments wrap around the joints and hold them together. Ligaments stretch when the bones move.

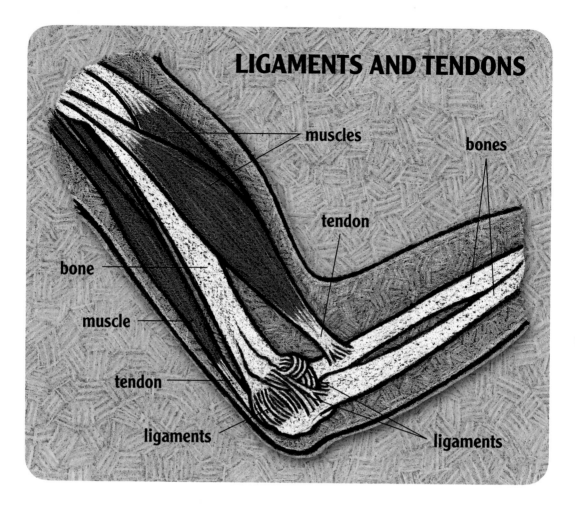

LIGAMENTS AND TENDONS

muscles

bones

tendon

bone

muscle

tendon

ligaments

ligaments

Muscles are attached to bones by narrow bands called tendons. Tendons are like strong strings at the ends of the muscles. They let the muscles pull the bones and make them move. You can see the tendons in the back of your hand move when you bend your fingers.

CHAPTER 5

HEALTHY BONES

Drinking milk helps to make your bones strong.
What other things can you do to help your bones?

Healthy bones are part of a healthy body. You can help keep your bones strong and healthy by eating good foods and getting enough exercise.

Your bones need vitamins and minerals to be strong. Milk and other dairy foods are good sources of the vitamins and minerals bones need.

Exercise helps your bones by keeping your muscles strong. It also keeps your joints moving well.

You can take care of the bones in your back by practicing good posture. When you stand and sit up straight you avoid hurting your back.

Your skeleton is an important part of a healthy body. You couldn't stand, walk, run, or eat without it.

Exercise is good for your bones and for the rest of your body.

ON SHARING A BOOK

When you share a book with a child, you show that reading is important. To get the most out of the experience, read in a comfortable, quiet place. Turn off the television and limit other distractions, such as telephone calls.

Be prepared to start slowly. Take turns reading parts of this book. Stop occasionally and discuss what you're reading. Talk about the photographs. If the child begins to lose interest, stop reading. When you pick up the book again, revisit the parts you have already read.

BE A VOCABULARY DETECTIVE

The word list on page 5 contains words that are important in understanding the topic of this book. Be word detectives and search for the words as you read the book together. Talk about what the words mean and how they are used in the sentence. Do any of these words have more than one meaning? You will find the words defined in a glossary on page 46.

WHAT ABOUT QUESTIONS?

Use questions to make sure the child understands the information in this book. Here are some suggestions:

> What did this paragraph tell us? What does this picture show? What do you think we'll learn about next? Why do you need bones in your body? What are the different kinds of joints that connect the bones? What can you do to keep your bones healthy? What is your favorite part of the book? Why?

If the child has questions, don't hesitate to respond with questions of your own, such as: What do *you* think? Why? What is it that you don't know? If the child can't remember certain facts, turn to the index.

INTRODUCING THE INDEX

The index helps readers find information without searching through the whole book. Turn to the index on page 48. Choose an entry such as *joints* and ask the child to use the index to find out what kind of joint the shoulder is. Repeat with as many entries as you like. Ask the child to point out the differences between an index and a glossary. (The index helps readers find information, while the glossary tells readers what words mean.)

LEARN MORE ABOUT
THE SKELETAL SYSTEM

BOOKS

Anderson, Karen C., and Stephen Cumbaa. *The Bones and Skeleton Gamebook.* New York : Workman Publishing Company, 1993. This book is packed with activities, quizzes, games, puzzles, and experiments exploring the human body and how it works.

Cumbaa, Stephen. *The Bones and Skeleton Book.* New York: Workman Publishing Company, 1992. This informative book about the bones and other body systems comes with an easy-to-assemble plastic skeleton model that snaps together easily.

Gray, Susan Heinrichs. *The Skeletal System.* Chanhassen, MN: Child's World, 2004. This book describes the skeletal system in a question-and-answer format.

LeVert, Suzanne. *Bones and Muscles.* New York: Benchmark Books, 2002. Learn how the bones and the muscles work together.

Maurer, Tracy. *Bones.* Vero Beach, FL: Rourke Corp., 1999. This book includes fun facts about the skeletal system.

WEBSITES
My Body
    http://www.kidshealth.org/kid/body/mybody.html
    This fun website has information on the systems of the human body, plus movies, games, and activities.

Pathfinders for Kids: The Skeletal System—The Bone Zone
    http://www.imcpl.org/kids/guides/health/skeletalsystem.html
    This Web page has a list of resources you can use to learn more about the skeletal system.

Skeletons and Bones at Enchanted Learning
    http://www.enchantedlearning.com/themes/skeleton.shtml
    This site has fun skeleton crafts, plus information about the skeletons of people, birds, and dinosaurs.

GLOSSARY

blood vessels: the tubes in the body through which blood flows

cartilage (KAR-tuh-lihj): a tough, white material that protects bones where they rub against each other

enamel (ih-NAM-uhl): the tough material on the outside of teeth. Enamel protects your teeth from wearing down as you chew.

joint: a place where two bones meet

ligaments (LIHG-uh-mehnts): strong, tough bands that connect bones

marrow: a soft, jellylike material found in the center of most bones. Yellow bone marrow stores fat. Red bone marrow makes blood cells.

nerves: fibers that carry messages between the brain and the rest of the body

organs: parts of the body that have a special purpose. The heart, lungs, and eyes are organs.

periosteum (PAIR-ee-OHS-tee-uhm): a thin layer of blood vessels and nerves that covers most of the surface of a bone. The periosteum helps the bone grow and repair itself.

skeleton: the framework of bones in the body

skull: the bony case that protects the brain and other organs of the head

spinal cord: the thick cord that is found inside the spine. The spinal cord is made up of many nerves.

spine: the row of bones that runs down the center of the back; backbone

tendons: tough bands that connect muscles to bones

vertebra (VUHR-tuh-bruh): one of the 33 bones of the spine

INDEX

Pages listed in **bold** type refer to photographs.

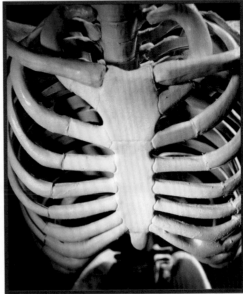